1989
To Liz,
with love!

HANNA'S HOG

HANNA'S HOG

by Jim
Aylesworth

illustrated by

Glen Rounds

Atheneum   1988   New York

Atheneum. Macmillan Publishing Company. 866 Third Avenue, New York, NY 10022
Collier Macmillan Canada, Inc.

Type set by V & M Graphics, New York City. Printed and bound by Toppan Printing Company, Japan.
Typography by Mary Ahern. First Edition.

10 9 8 7 6 5 4 3 2 1

Library of Congress Cataloging-in-Publication Data

Aylesworth, Jim.   Hanna's hog.

SUMMARY: Hanna finds a way to protect her hog and chickens from a thieving neighbor.
[1. Mountain life—Fiction] I. Rounds, Glen,
1906-   ill.   II. Title.
PZ7.A983Han   1988   [E]   87-11559
ISBN 0-689-31367-5

To Ellen, with love.

J. A.

HANNA BRODIE lived back on the mountain. She raised chickens for the eggs, kept bees for the honey, and she worked a big garden. She also had a fine fat hog that she let run loose in the woods.

Now most hogs that run loose soon turn to wild, but not Hanna's hog. Hanna kept her hog as tame as a pup by saving back things that hogs are partial to . . . like melon rinds and cobs from roastin' ears, and such.

And once a day, she'd call it in.

"Soowee! Soopig! Soo pig pig pig!", and that hog would come running. Hanna never had a bit of trouble with it.

As a matter of fact, about the only kind of trouble Hanna did have was the human kind. His name was Kenny Jackson, and he lived about two miles away on the other side of the woods.

The trouble was that Hanna kept coming up short on chickens. And although she hadn't caught him at it, Hanna was powerful certain that Kenny Jackson was doing it. But every time Hanna asked him about it, he just looked uncomfortable and tried to put the blame on a fox, or a chicken hawk or something. Hanna didn't believe it.

The last straw came one afternoon when Hanna went out,
as usual, to call in her hog.

"*Soowee! Soopig! Soo pig pig pig!*"

No hog!

She called again. Louder.

"*Soowee! Soopig! Soo pig pig pig!*"

Still no hog!

Hanna was fit to be tied.

After searching high and low most of that night and half the next day to make sure her hog hadn't just run off or took sick or something, Hanna decided to go visit Kenny Jackson. A few chickens is one thing, but a fat hog is altogether a different matter. Something had to be done!

When Hanna drove up into Kenny's yard, Kenny was sitting on the porch.

"I've come up missing my hog," said Hanna. "You ain't seen her up this way have you?"

Kenny answered real sweet-like,
    "Why no, Hanna. I sure ain't. There ain't been a hog
around this place in years as a matter of fact."

Hanna looked him straight in the eye and didn't say any-
thing. It made Kenny sort of nervous, so he kept on talking.

"But if you're missing your hog, maybe that fellar that was
through here last week was right after all."

"Right about what?" asked Hanna.

"Well, I didn't believe it at the time," said Kenny. "But that fellar told me he saw sign of bear back yonder in the woods. Maybe he was right. Maybe a bear took your hog. I'd be real careful if I was you."

Hanna knew that a bear hadn't been seen in that county for more than fifty years, so she found Kenny's tale a bit hard to swallow. But not knowing what else to do just then, she started up the truck, thanked Kenny kindly for the warning, and headed for home.

On the way out of the yard, however, Hanna caught sight of hog tracks by the barn, and she knew that Kenny was lying.

"That devil!" Hanna said to herself. Then she went on home to think things over.

She spent the rest of the day in her garden, fuming about her hog and cussing Kenny Jackson.

By evening, she had herself a plan.

When it got dark, she took a piece of broken rake and a bit of rope, and snuck on over to Kenny's place, quiet as she could be. She slipped up into the yard where she could see the house, sat down behind a rhododendron bush, and waited.

Before long, Kenny came out, walked over to the out-house, and went inside.

It was just what Hanna was waiting on.

Quiet, quiet, quiet, Hanna crept up and started making growling noises in the back of her throat.

" . . . *rrrrr* . . . *rrrrr* . . . "

And with that busted rake, she started scratching the back of that outhouse, gouging claw marks into the wood.

From the inside, it all sounded like a bear out there, sure enough! And Kenny was plum scared to death! . . . too scared to holler! . . . too scared to run!

So he just stayed in there, holding the door shut with all his might.

In the meantime, Hanna went over to the barn, found a spot where she wouldn't leave a track, scratched some claw marks on the side of the barn, and broke off a few boards. Then, quick as a wink, she put the rope on her hog and led it off through the woods to home.

Hanna was so tickled pink to get her hog back, that she laughed right out loud to the moon and danced a little jig there in the yard. But before she went inside to bed, she took that piece of rake and made a few claw marks on the side of her truck.

Bright and early the next morning, Hanna drove back over to see Kenny. He was out on the porch and there was a shotgun leaning against the post.

"I come to thank you for warning me about that bear," said Hanna. "Last night, I was out in the woods hunting for my hog when the bear comes tearing out of the brush. I just barely had time to jump in the truck. He'd a got me sure if I hadn't had an eye out for him. That fellar you was talking with was right after all, just like you said."

Kenny came down into the yard and
ran his finger across the marks on Hanna's truck.

"I had the same trouble over this way," said Kenny. "That
bear had me holed up most of the night. I thought I was a
goner . . . busted up my barn too. Looking for something to
eat, I reckon."

"My, my, my," said Hanna. "Looks like we're both lucky to be alive!"

"Right you are about that!" said Kenny.

From that day on, Hanna stopped coming up short on chickens. She guessed it was because Kenny was too scared to go into the woods.

And Hanna was right. Truth is, he didn't even go to the outhouse without taking the shotgun.

And as for the hog, all Hanna had to do was to call,
"*Soowee! Soopig! Soo pig pig pig!*" and it would come
running.

. . . Every time!